FOLLOW IN THE FUTURE WITH THE SHADOW

INTERNATIONAL INTERGALACTICAL SPACE SECRET SERVICE (IISSS)

GEORGIY SERGEYEVICH GARBUZ

Published 2024

Printed in the United States of America

First Edition

ISBN (softcover): 978-1-963380-34-7
ISBN (e-book): 978-1-963380-33-0

For information, address:

Holzer Books LLC
8 The Green, Ste. A
Dover, Delaware 19901 USA

For information about special discounts available for bulk purchases, sales promotions, and educational needs, contact:

info@holzerbooksllc.com
+1 (888) 901-7776

THE VISION OF
THE INTERNATIONAL
INTERGALACTICAL SPACE
SECRET SERVICE

Life is a strange thing; it gives you so many opportunities. It depends on you what you choose and how you live your life. You can be part of the legal system or turn into an outlaw to make money, fulfill your desires, and make your wishes come true in the real world. But it always gets controlled and hunted by different government agencies. Keeping control is a really hard job and requires too much money to recruit special and supportive agents in the country. This ensures that all happenings in the world are under control, and the agency knows all information long before it happens. This allows them to take the required actions to provide a safe society for people and kids. This is very important because there are 7.9 billion people in the world, each with a different mindset, and everybody takes their own actions.

What they planned, even if it was illegal business or required breaking the law and becoming outlaws in the system, people do it anyway. They do it to make money, even if it means injuring innocent people and kids. This is all about money and power in the world. To achieve their goals, they need finance; they need money to execute their plans because it all involves financing, technology, people, and other resources.

The first rule in secret operations is to check financial transactions of the subject to understand how it was financed. This can reveal who is responsible for events in the world and who ordered such actions—be it companies, people, or countries. In this world, there are many crazy people who undertake the most dangerous operations. They are always funded by different organizations and groups of people who believe that what they are doing is better for the world or for themselves.

Today we are going to talk about the control of space. I want to share my idea of opening a collaborative effort with America, Russia, India, Germany, China, and England as space leaders, along with all the countries around the world. This would be an international intergalactic Space Secret Service, the highest worldwide international space agency. It would provide safety for people in the countries of the world and on other planets.

Everything out there in the cosmos and on other planets would receive special attention from these space agencies to ensure the safety of innocent people, especially children. Children are the flowers of life and need to be educated. They are the ones who will stay after we leave this world, continuing the circle of life, generation by generation, from father to son, from son to grandson.

This is a good time to establish a new international intergalactic space agency and start educating kids in space school academies. This will ensure that in 10 years, there will be enough people, such as special agents, astronauts, space doctors, space engineers, and many other professionals needed for our planet to conduct research and colonize space and the planets around the universe and galaxies.

We are the people who believe that the prosperity of a country and its people starts with education. The more people who receive professional education, the more prosperous the country becomes.

We are the people who want to lay the foundation of the International Intergalactic Space Secret Service through the education of talented kids. These kids, with good grades, will be granted free education at Garbuz Space School Academies. After finishing 8th grade, they will advance to the Garbuz Space Academies to complete their education and become future professional employees.

We are the people who believe in a better and more prosperous future for our country, our world, and our people.

The International Intergalactic Space Secret Service is a special agency designed to ensure the safety and prosperity of people around the world and across the galaxies. It will be founded by the future National Intergalactic Space Federation Government and based on the projects of Georgiy Sergeyevich Garbuz, the founder of this initiative. Garbuz, a man who loves children, is dedicated to doing everything in his power to ensure foster kids are educated and prosper in the future.

The idea of creating a space agency emerged in 2007 during a time of economic depression, as a means to boost the economy. The vision is for all member countries to fall under the leadership of America, Russia, China, Germany, India, and England, coming together to conduct research and colonize planets in the universe. Each country will have a head of the agency within their territory, typically the existing president, under the overarching leadership of the President of the International Intergalactic Space Federation. This structure will actually increase the power of each president, benefiting the prosperity of their respective countries and their people.

The most important goal of the International Intergalactic Space Secret Service is to ensure the prosperity of the people and to establish a stable economy on Earth. The purpose of the IISF is to ensure the safety of people and children on the planet and in the galaxies, securing what is beyond our atmosphere. However, their responsibilities extend beyond space; the agency is also responsible for the safety and prosperous life on our planet.

The project will start from Earth and, step by step, establish livable environments on other planets as research and colonization begin. Together with all the countries involved, we predict that if the project starts now, within the next 10 years we will begin colonizing and researching Mars and the Moon. We will have enough technology to deliver colonists to these planets and bring back natural resources to Earth for corporations and people.

It is important to understand what natural resources each planet has, as different planets have different atmospheres. By researching these planets, we will likely discover many new natural minerals previously unknown to us. This is the first step for the agency: to establish a functioning organization worldwide and start researching other planets.

The headquarters of the International Intergalactic Space Secret Service will be in Minnesota, United States, with 49 million special space agents around the world. This large number of agents will require significant financing, which will start from Georgiy Sergeyevich Garbuz's projects. This initiative is expected to bring in multi-trillion dollar revenues to the government and the people. The project was created specifically to educate foster kids and involve them in the agency's work.

This project is inspired by "Lyubov" - love for the children - to create projects in various fields such as science, technology, medicine, and more. The aim is to help establish the agency around the world, forming teams ready to work on these initiatives. We ask governments to direct tax revenue into the project, which grows every year with new ideas and creations. The goal is to encourage more people to start new businesses, benefiting the country's environment and providing benefits for its people.

While some may initially view ideas like legalizing non-addictive marijuana and prostitution worldwide as crazy, the potential profits and revenue they could generate for countries become apparent over time. This influx of money could significantly boost the economy and benefit the people. Every human deserves stability from this money, which could provide benefits like free education and healthcare, essential for starting life in the future.

This promise to the government and the people ensures enough financing for programs that need to be funded worldwide. It's a big commitment to the country, the world, and the people, especially the children.

To establish space school academies and provide free grants to talented kids, funds will be directed from the science projects, technologies, medical inventions, and medicines of Georgiy Sergeyevich Garbuz. These resources will ensure enough funds to educate 17 million kids every year. As the project gains momentum and the team is established, it will expand further, progressing step by step.

Another crucial function of the International Intergalactical Space Secret Service will be to combat internet identity theft, crypto scams, copyright infringement, and other forms of online fraud that result in multimillion-dollar losses every day. Currently, the law enforcement agencies like the police, FBI, and their international counterparts, face challenges due to jurisdictional issues and the time it takes to coordinate across different countries' legal systems.

However, the International Intergalactical Space Federation will change this dynamic by having control over all satellites and stations worldwide. By cooperating closely with local police and federal bureaus in each country and having accounts established under their jurisdiction, the agency will be able to swiftly respond to reports of fraud. They can promptly submit and prosecute cases in every country, ensuring that the perpetrators are apprehended and brought to justice. This proactive approach will significantly enhance global efforts to combat cybercrime and protect individuals and businesses from online threats.

INTERNATIONAL INTERGALACTICAL SPACE SECRET SERVICE

S pace is the uncharted frontier that humanity has relentlessly sought to explore. Today, millions of people observe the cosmos through telescopes, but regrettably, some individuals exploit this fascination for fraudulent purposes. Every day, millions of people fall victim to these thieves, suffering financial losses and more. Yet, there is no institution equipped to investigate such matters on an international scale and deliver concrete results.

The International Intergalactic Space Secret Service was conceived to address this pressing need. Its mission: to safeguard and ensure national stability across planets, space, and countries. The agency's founders hail from five global powers – America, Russia, China, England, India, and Germany. Each country is tasked with the security of the assigned territories in both space and their homelands. With over 17 million active space agents and the support of 7.5 billion citizens, this agency stands poised to provide comprehensive planetary security and deliver critical national safety information.

This agency is dedicated to gathering crucial intelligence and collaborating with other agencies worldwide to prevent the most dangerous threats facing our planet. For instance, in recruiting supporting country space agents, it would require $2.6552 trillion annually from the 331.9 million citizens of the USA and $286.8 billion from Russia's 143.4 million supporting agents, with similar calculations for the rest of the world.

Funding for this monumental endeavor can be sourced from dedicated taxes on the legalized marijuana and prostitution industries. The legalization of these practices globally can significantly enhance the safety of our world, our countries, and our people. This approach allows every individual to contribute through their work, provision of information, and compensation. In turn, each country can afford to provide free healthcare, education, and other essential services to its citizens, fostering a cooperative environment for space exploration and planetary colonization.

Key Aspects of the Project:

1. **Financing:** Funding from the legalized marijuana and prostitution industries will support this endeavor.

2. **Selection of Professional Employees and Specialists:** The agency will carefully select and employ experts in relevant fields.

3. **Acquisition of Special Materials and Technologies:** The project will invest in advanced materials and technologies required for its implementation.

4. **Government Oversight:** The establishment of these agencies will be carried out under governmental supervision.

The revenues generated from the legalized industries will be channeled towards the Garbuz Space Academy Program, founded by Georgiy S. Garbuz. This visionary project, initiated in 2007, aims to build the National Garbuz Space Academy and affiliated schools across the globe, providing opportunities for foster care children and underprivileged youth to receive a quality education.

PERSONAL EXPERIENCES AND RESEARCH

Our advocacy for action isn't just based on belief; it's supported by research indicating that millions of people lose significant sums annually, ranging from $35,000 to $75,000, falling victim to international scam schemes. These losses reflect in tax declarations, resulting in the loss of trillions of dollars in tax revenue for countries.

This money is crucial for funding projects that bring tangible benefits to the people. Cryptocurrency, being a relatively new digital currency, lacks adequate government regulations, making it an easy target for criminals seeking to exploit individuals looking to invest.

Our research, which began in 2015, highlights that the internet is heavily utilized by thieves. They often masquerade as trusted contacts, exploiting personal connections to gain victims' trust before exploiting them.

It happened to me. A girl named Amy contacted me and struck up a conversation. She seemed to know a lot about me, my lifestyle, and what I do. She encouraged me to invest money in cryptocurrency, promising good profits. Intrigued, I decided to invest a few thousand dollars in "trusted" websites. I opened an account and bought Shiba Inu for $5,000, a cryptocurrency I found myself. This wasn't her idea, but she persuaded me to open an account on a website and buy a cryptocurrency called ICPII. The website seemed legitimate, and I purchased $10,000 worth of ICPII. The market fluctuated, but it looked promising, especially since I owned Shiba Inu and monitored it daily. Shiba Inu rose to 0.000015. and ICPII to 0.000001. Everything seemed fine, and the investment appeared to be doing well.

She inspired me to invest more money in ICPII, putting an additional $15,000 while still working my job and occasionally trading. Being busy, I relied on a trusted analyst to provide insights on market trends. I paid them a 10 percent commission from the profits, which worked well for both parties.

For six months, I didn't see my trusted analyst, so I turned to Amy, offering her the same deal to analyze the market for meonce we finished investing in ICPII. Surpisingly, after six months, Shiba Inu had risen to 0.00046, and ICPII had increased to $269 per token - a remarkable but unbelievable result.

Finally, my analyst returned from vacation, and I showed him the cryptocurrencies, hoping he could provide some analysis. After explaining everything, I went to work. A few days later, he called me while I was conducting research on using art to treat depression. (It turned out to be effective, as my research revealed that art is essential for relaxing the brain and combating depression, especially during times of uncertainty.)

He called me, and we met at a restaurant. We talked and discussed how cryptocurrency is new and gaining acceptance as a legitimate form of payment. While Shiba Inu seemed promising, he expressed doubts about ICPII and the website, suggesting it could be a scam. He warned me that the investment was risky, with a 50/50 chance of success or failure.

I mentioned my research for the International Intergalactical Space Secret Service, which piqued his interest. As I discussed it further, he suggested trying to withdraw the money invested in ICPII. Amy informed me that I needed to pay $5,000 to withdraw the funds, which raised suspicions.

Despite my doubts, I paid the $5,000, and they transferred the ICPII to a different site where I could sell them. However, I soon realized it was a scam. Nevertheless, it provided valuable information for my research and would aid in catching international thieves in the future. Although ICPII skyrocketed to $5,000, Amy insisted on investing more, claiming it would double soon. This time, I had a different plan - to gather more information about her.

So I told her I didn't have available funds anymore to invest, but if she loaned me money, I'd give her 500 percent of the profit from the amount. Surprisingly, she agreed, and I provided her with my trusted digital wallet address. She transferred $35,000 from her account, which I monitored. I invested this money in ICPII and waited. After a few months, Amy insisted on investing more money. I agreed, and she transferred $25,000, this time using a different account number.

Having multiple accounts made it easier to gather more information about her, including her bank accounts. I always make sure to document details and check IDs under the camera, making it easier to identify her.

As months passed, I continued conversations with Amy, asking for more information. She revealed that she basically lived in Hong Kong, China, which posed significant risks due to the severe penalties for fraud and theft in China. This made her an easy target for agents from different countries for various reasons. To avoid being caught, she needed a strong cover, possibly working for a double agency in a different country.

As time passed, the value of ICPII surged to $1,000 per coin, resulting in an unbelievable profit of $160 million from my initial investment of $75,000. With such significant gains, I decided to conclude my research on Amy and attempted to withdraw my money.

I reached out to her, but received no response, which seemed typical of thieves. However, the following week, the ICPII began to fluctuate, and the day after, the value of ICPII plummeted to $300. By the following week, the website had been shut down and closed, leaving everyone who invested money at a loss. People began writing reviews labeling it a fraud, and Amy, who had inspired many to invest, was at the center of the inquiries.

Shockingly, there were no institutions equipped to investigate cryptocurrency fraud. Typically, individuals would report such incidents to the police of the Federal Bureau of Investigation. This is exactly what I did - I visited them, filled out a report, and opened a fraud case.

Meanwhile, I continued monitoring Amy's activity on her dating site profile, where she had already begun promoting a different new cryptocurrency. Through reading reviews on ICPII, I discovered that she had engaged with at least 40 other individuals who invested money in ICPII.

Most of the victims were from the United States of America, including myself. However, amidst this setback, my research led to many ideas and strategies regarding what needs to be accomplished with the International Intergalactical Space Secret Service.

One idea that emerged was the crucial first step of the International Intergalactical Space Secret Service to combat international thieves across the world. This initiative is essential before we embark on research, development, and colonization of other planets in the universe. It's vital for people to trust in conducting online activities, especially investments, without fear of losing money to internet fraudsters.

Despite the setback of my loss, my research progressed well, leading me to contemplate the interconnectedness of these individuals and the possibility of a large criminal organization. Their seemingly intimate knowledge of my life was unsettling, but it spurred me to delve deeper into my research.

While continuing my studies on the psychological treatment of depression, I also explored alternative avenues. Reflecting on my experience with depression treatment, I discovered the therapeutic benefits of art painting. Engaging in painting not only occupied my time but also diverted my thoughts away from negative tendencies associated with depression. I found it to be a cost-effective method, requiring minimal investment in materials but providing days of engagement and excitement.

Using this newfound focus, I redirected my research towards investigating online prostitution thefts. This aligned with my project's aim to advocate for the legalization of prostitution worldwide, believing it could positively impact the economy. However, I recognized the complexities involved in legalizing such activities and understood the necessity for a well-planned approach to ensure its success, unlike the rushed legalization of marijuana in the USA, which lacked consideration for associated issues like depression.

It seemed like integrating this approach into the International Intergalactic Space Secret Service project could prove beneficial, given my experience in identifying online scammers. Through my research, I had observed a prevalent pattern: out of every ten women on dating sites, seven would eventually ask for money.

To counteract this, I implemented a strategic approach. When they requested money, I always responded by offering to pay for services, emphasizing that I would only send money if they provided the agreed-upon service or product. Typically, they would inquire about the type of service required.

In response, I would openly state that I was willing to pay for sexual services or research. When asked about the payment rate, I would specify $150 per hour. Remarkably, over a thousand women in my research had expressed willingness to provide services for payment.

I adopted this strategy as a means to fulfill my natural needs without complicating my life with relationship issues before settling down. By clearly communicating the terms of payment for services rendered, I mitigated the risk of being reported for sexual harassment. The agreement was clear: payment for services provided, with no questions asked - just a straightforward transaction of money for sexual services.

It's true, the internet can be a minefield of scams. That's why it's crucial to rely on trusted individuals or those you know personally, especially when engaging in online transactions. As I continued my painting sessions, a message popped up on Messenger from someone named Emily Taylor, requesting friendship. We started chatting, and being a social person, I engaged in friendly conversation.

However, my expectations were swiftly dashed when on the second day of chatting, Emily asked me for money to buy underwear. Like with previous encounters, I reiterated that I only paid for services. Surprisingly, she agreed to provide a sexual service. However, I hadn't intended to invite her over, so she proposed sending a video of herself masturbating, which she claimed to have made especially for me. She requested that I buy her a dildo for $30, ostensibly for research purposes.

Curious, I obliged, and the next day, I received the video. Given my life experience, I suspected that she was involved in pornography and possibly prostitution. It appeared that she was operating within the legal adult industry, though likely engaged in illicit activities on the side.

Despite the initial transaction, I sought to learn more about her beyond just purchasing a sex video or availing myself of her services. Over time, I continued to send her money for these videos, but during our conversations, she expressed an interest in painting. I shared that I, too, painted for my research on treating depression. Eventually, she revealed that she also painted and hoped to open her own studio someday.

It became intriguing when she shared her paintings with me; they were beautiful and professionally done, resembling the work of someone who had completed art college. This piqued my interest, and I began discussing my scientific work, explaining its purpose and functionality. She expressed enthusiasm for my project and expressed a desire to join once it became an official research endeavor. This arrangement suited me better than simply sending her money every week; I preferred to purchase a painting from her rather than send money without receiving anything in return.

Then, the day arrived when she informed me that her mother was ill and needed $100 for medication. I declined to provide the money but inquired about the price of her paintings, as I wished to commission some from her. She quoted $500, to which I agreed. I sent her a picture of my mother and requested that she paint her, promising to purchase the painting upon completion. She used different accounts to receive the payment, but within a week, she completed the painting and showed me a fading picture of it. Despite the fading, I admired her skill and eagerly anticipated receiving the painting, as it was important to me to have a memento of my mother in my bedroom, painted by someone else.

However, the following day, she informed me that her mother had passed away and she needed money for the funeral expenses. I proposed that she send me the painting, and in return, I would send her $150, which she agreed to. I fulfilled my end of the agreement by sending her the money.

The next day, she messaged me with instructions to receive a delivery through email. I was informed that I needed to pay $8,000 for one-day shipping of the package. This request seemed suspicious, especially considering that the girl seemed solely focused on her painting skills, and many of my friends were interested in ordering from her. Sensing a scam, I decided to report the situation to the police and opened a fraud case.

Despite my attempts to reach out to her and suggest alternative ways to earn money, she did not respond.

THE IMPORTANCE OF COMBATING ONLINE FRAUD

A lthough I incurred a loss of $3,500 in my research, it provided valuable insights into the workings of online thieves. It became apparent that these individuals operated as part of a large criminal network, sharing information about their victims to perpetrate scams.

This experience reinforced the necessity of the International Intergalactic Space Secret Service, highlighting the ongoing need to combat crime across planets and ensure the safety of people. As the agency continues its development, it is crucial to enlist professionals from every country to contribute to research and program development.

The people I know and collaborate with understand the importance of our operation. It's progressing well, fueled by the understanding that waiting for change won't bring results. Most are committed to investigations that hold significant importance for the world. Crime persists and evolves; it's a constant battle. People are always drawn to easy money, often resorting to breaking the law. While I've suffered losses in my research, I've also gained insights into how to prevent and apprehend criminals.

The ideas generated through my research will greatly contribute to the agency's mission. Life presents choices, and people have the power to create with their minds. I've observed how interconnected everyone is, prompting me to delve into researching celebrities and artists as part of my efforts to combat depression. I've created numerous artworks and even composed a song titled "Hello Father." This song, born from the depths of sorrow and love, holds immense significance to me, and sharing it with the public feels like a crucial step.

I took the first step towards selecting the singer for my song by engaging with various artists online. Among them, I found Jenifer, whose music I deeply admired for its psychological impact. Music has a unique ability to evoke emotions - love, longing, anger - and singers, as conduits of this art, hold a special place in society, warranting collaboration with governments to ensure global safety.

I reached out to Jenifer through a private fan page, aware of the interconnectedness of such platforms. Following numerous interactions, they informed me that to communicate directly with Jenifer, I needed to purchase a fan membership card worth $1,000. Despite initial hesitations, I proceeded with the purchase, eager to discuss the possibility of her singing my song.

However, my optimism waned when I realized that every fan page I engaged with began pushing me to buy their membership cards, each claiming to be the sole authentic page. This revelation exposed a pervasive online scam, wherein celebrity fan pages with millions of followers defrauded unsuspecting individuals. Despite this setback, I resolved to delve deeper into the workings of these scammers for my international intergalactic space secret service project, regardless of the cost.

My decision to provide personal information upon purchasing the fan membership card proved prescient. While discussions about my song progressed, they tactfully requested weekly donations of $50 to support orphaned children. Despite my altruistic intentions, I recognized the potential risks involved and the absence of receipts for my donations. Nonetheless, these experiences provided invaluable insights into the extent of financial losses people endure daily, reinforcing the importance of my research.

CELEBRITY SCAMS AND THE "CATCH PRO" OPERATION

I was taken aback when Jenifer began discussing marriage, especially since I knew she was already married with two children. It was a clear indication of fraud. Curiosity led me to read reviews about her alleged new husband, further confirming my suspicions. Nonetheless, I continued observing the interactions between the five different Jenifer fan pages, noting how they spammed each other and shared more information.

To test my strategy, I decided to share my business plan with her, curious to see her response. Each fan page had its own set of individuals who were willing to pay 20% of their earnings to Jenifer. As I shared my project, they all expressed interest and eagerness to develop their own space corporations. It was a testament to the success of my strategy, as they focused solely on the potential revenue it could generate.

Seeing their enthusiasm, I knew my plan was working effectively. They became engrossed in the project, eager to embark on their own ventures.

It's common for them to request a $50 donation to orphan kids, under the guise of helping children in need. While aiding orphaned kids is crucial, it's uncertain if the donations actually reach them. Often, they ask for gift cards, a common tactic used by fraudsters.

Despite not receiving receipts for my donations, I decided to wait and see what would unfold next.

Each day, I received notifications to join various Jenifer fan pages, all soliciting money for membership. Despite informing them that I had already paid, I continued to receive spam messages. They began spamming each other, claiming exclusivity as the only authentic Jenifer page. I found myself engaged with five different pages, all exhibiting the same behavior. It was clear evidence of spam, but for my research, I needed to delve deeper to uncover their true intentions.

As I anticipated, a new proposition swiftly arrived. Jenifer, who had previously offered to marry me, now insisted that we needed a house costing $500 a week. I declined, explaining that I couldn't send money for a house without meeting her in person.

Marrying a celebrity actress is no easy feat, especially if you're just a fan. While most fans would eagerly agree, my intentions were different. I simply wanted her to sing my song and potentially collaborate on an international intergalactical space project. I knew she was intriguing, but her involvement in soliciting money from orphaned kids hinted at ulterior motives.

As time passed, she began insisting that I open a trading account on cheapertrade. com, promising significant profits that could benefit my project. Despite my usual caution with new sites, given the prevalence of fraud in the crypto space, I agreed to open an account since it aligned with my research on frauds for the International Intergalactical Space Secret Service project. She provided me with Susan's messenger for financing, along with the website link, and I invested the money to observe the outcome. It didn't take long to realize it was a fraud; as soon as she made a $5,000 profit, I expressed my intention to withdraw it to test the account's legitimacy. However, it quickly became apparent that something was amiss when she informed me that I needed to pay a $1,300 withdrawal fee. Despite my suspicions, I transferred the money by the end of the week.

The pattern repeated itself: every time I attempted to withdraw my profits, she demanded additional fees. Each time, I complied, hoping to retrieve my money, but to no avail. It became a futile game of constantly paying more fees, with no returns. Frustrated by the endless requests for money, I decided to enact my strategy. When she asked for more funds, I informed her that I couldn't comply, prompting her to contact Jenifer.

Jennifer started messaging me again because she recommended me to her. I explained that I didn't have any money, but proposed a deal: if she paid the withdrawal fee, she would receive 50% of my profits for her kids. She declined, claiming she had already spent all her money on her children, but promised to help next month.

To expose the fraud, I went to the police and filed a report, waiting to see what would happen next. The case remained open, and it turned into a waiting game to see how they would try to extract more money from me.

Day after day, Jennifer introduced me to her celebrity friends, all of whom discussed Susan and the need to pay the withdrawal fee to access the money. It became evident that this fraud involved a team effort, with at least 20 people contacting me about Susan and Jennifer. While some might argue that Jennifer is unaware of the fraud, the reality is that she benefits from it. She has potentially lost billions of dollars, as each of her fans would pay significant amounts to connect with her and support orphan kids. She is aware of this but struggles to make a choice.

Considering the scale of this operation, it highlights the immense task ahead for the International Intergalactical Space Secret Service. With offices in every city, it would be easier to catch thieves, terrorists, and other criminals.

Fraud is a lucrative business that will never cease entirely. People are drawn to easy money, even at the risk of imprisonment. To combat it effectively, there needs to be an incentive for people to actively pursue the thieves. Thus, we created a secret operation called "Catch Pro" for the International Intergalactical Space Secret Service.

It's time for action, and I can assure you it's going to work! As soon as we receive a report of fraud, investigators swing into action. They meticulously examine all the transfer accounts involved in receiving or withdrawing the money, regardless of the country they're in. They also scrutinize emails and messenger conversations to ensure we catch all the individuals involved in this organized crime.

This is crucial because these criminals never operate alone. Once our agency identifies the culprits, we issue wanted orders to the cities where they reside and operate. From there, our local offices send the orders to the police, instructing them to arrest the thieves.

Once apprehended, the legal team contacts the victims and initiates a fraud case in court. Typically, lawyers take 33% of the winnings from a successful case. This incentivizes them to work diligently to secure compensation for the victims who have lost their hard-earned money.

The aim is to not only recover the stolen funds but also ensure that the perpetrator faces consequences for their actions. They receive jail time and are required to pay compensation to the victim and the city. This serves as a deterrent and sends a clear message that fraudulent activities will not be tolerated.

With these measures in place, everyone is motivated to identify and apprehend those involved in fraud and theft.

SPACE EXPLORATION AND RESOURCE MANAGEMENT

The International Intergalactic Space Secret Service places a high priority on ensuring the safety of space and the inhabitants of galaxies. Beyond Earth's atmosphere, our jurisdiction extends to satellites orbiting the planet, which play a crucial role in gathering information about us. However, when these satellites malfunction or become obsolete, they pose a significant threat as space debris. Therefore, one of our primary objectives is to clean up space debris to ensure that space territory remains clear for spacecraft navigation.

To achieve this goal, we will need new garbage space ships equipped with advanced technology to effectively clean up space debris. The Commander of the International Intergalactical Space Secret Service, who is the Former Secretary of Defense, will oversee the establishment of this operation and ensure that it operates efficiently and effectively.

This operation will require a substantial amount of resources, including personnel and financing. Funding will come from the various scientific projects initiated by Georgy Sergeyevich Garbuz before the establishment of the International Intergalactic Space Federation. With a 6% taxation rate and 1.92% from global sales collected by the IISF, there will be sufficient funds to support the space agency's activities, including building spacecraft, conducting research, and colonizing planets.

Additionally, the International Intergalactical Space Federation will focus on establishing communication channels with every country to foster business opportunities and gather important information. This will be crucial for the success of our space exploration efforts.

One of the essential aspects of space exploration is ensuring the survival of astronauts in hostile environments. Therefore, the International Intergalactical Space Federation will prioritize research into providing essential resources such as air and water in space. This includes developing technologies to extract water from celestial bodies and creating life support systems to generate breathable air.

Furthermore, to encourage interest and participation in space exploration, the International Intergalactical Space Federation plans to establish the Garbuz Space School Academies for youth aged 14-18 and the Garbuz Space Academy for individuals of all ages. These academies will provide free education financed by Georgy Sergeyevich Garbuz's scientific and technological projects. Additionally, tax revenue will be directed towards providing free grants for foster kids and children with excellent grades, ensuring equal access to educational opportunities.

EDUCATION AND THE FUTURE OF SPACE EXPLORATION

Providing every child with access to free education is indeed crucial for shaping a better future and ensuring equal opportunities for all. The vision for the International Intergalactical Space Secret Service to establish Space School Academies reflects this commitment to nurturing the next generation of leaders and innovators.

empowering individuals to pursue their passions, develop their talents, and contribute meaningfully to society. By offering free education through Space School Academies, the International Intergalactical can inspire children to explore their interests in space exploration, science, technology, and other fields.

Moreover, investing in education is an investment in the future of our planet and beyond. By equipping children with the necessary skills and knowledge, we enable them to tackle the challenges of tomorrow, whether on Earth or in space. This initiative aligns with the the International Intergalactical's mission to ensure the safety and prosperity of humanity across galaxies.

Furthermore, by providing free education, we can break the cycle of poverty and inequality, opening doors to opportunities that were previously inaccessible to many. Every child deserves the chance to dream big and pursue their aspirations, regardless of their background or financial circumstances.

In essence, the establishment of Space School Academies represents a significant step towards building a brighter and more inclusive future for all. By investing in education, we invest in the potential of every child to become a leader, an innovator, and a positive force for change in the world.

The for the future of space exploration is ambitious and inspiring. Establishing a strong community within the International Intergalactic Space Secret Service is essential for accomplishing its mission of exploring the universe and unlocking its secrets.

Space indeed holds countless mysteries and opportunities waiting to be explored and researched. From uncovering the secrets of distant galaxies to discovering new resources and potential habitats on Mars and beyond, the journey into space promises to revolutionize our understanding of the cosmos and its potential for humanity.

By harnessing the collective expertise and resources of nations around the world, the International Space Secret Service can pave the way for unprecedented advancements in space exploration and development. This includes training astronauts, astrophysicists, aeronautics experts, and other professionals who will lead the charge into the unknown.

Moreover, establishing international intergalactic space corporations will be crucial for driving economic growth and sustainability in space exploration endeavors. These corporations, with guidance from the International Space Secret Service, can spearhead initiatives to establish life on other planets, exploit natural resources, and foster interplanetary trade and commerce.

Every country's participation in this endeavor is vital, and the International Space Secret Service plays a central role in ensuring coordination and cooperation among nations. By empowering individuals and corporations to contribute to space exploration, the International Intergalactical Space Secret can catalyze a new era of human progress and discovery.

Overall, the vision underscores the importance of international collaboration, innovation, and exploration in shaping the future of humanity's presence in space. Through the efforts of the International Space Secret Service and its partners, we can unlock the full potential of the universe and secure a prosperous future for generations to come.

THE NATIONAL GARBUZ SPACE ACADEMY TRUST CORPORATION

The establishment of the National Garbuz Space Academy Trust Corporation, known as "Uslovie," will mark a significant milestone in the pursuit of space exploration and education. This corporation, dedicated to generating multitrillion-dollar revenues, embodies a commitment to using its profits for the betterment of society, particularly for foster kids and underprivileged children worldwide.

Under the visionary leadership of Georgiy Sergeyevich Garbuz, the promise of providing free grants for education in Space Academies will be realized. Through relentless dedication and innovation, Garbuz has developed groundbreaking technologies and medical advancements that not only push the boundaries of space exploration but also benefit humanity in profound ways.

The focus on educating children from diverse backgrounds reflects a profound belief in the transformative power of education. By offering opportunities for children to study in Space Academies and pursue careers in space-related professions, the Uslovie Corporation aims to empower the next generation of leaders, scientists, and explorers.

Moreover, by directing tax revenue towards grants for foster kids and academically excellent students, the Corporation ensures that no child is left behind. This commitment to inclusivity and social responsibility underscores the ethos of the International Intergalactical Space Secret Service and its dedication to creating a better world for all.

Through the tireless efforts of Garbuz and his team, the dream of providing hope and opportunities to children in need becomes a reality. As the first wave of agents is trained and prepared to embark on their mission, they carry with them the promise of a brighter future for humanity, guided by the values of integrity, innovation, and compassion.

GLOBAL COOPERATION AND RESOURCE EXPLORATION

How the world operates today is centered around business endeavors, where individuals strive to pursue their passions and contribute to society. This includes providing children with the opportunity to choose their desired professions, allowing them to lead fulfilling lives, contribute to their communities, and pursue their aspirations. The International Intergalactical Space Secret Service plays a crucial role in turning these aspirations into reality by ensuring the safety of space borders and facilitating life on various planets. Moreover, it prepares humanity for interplanetary travel and colonization by developing essential technologies, spacecraft, and infrastructure.

The initial focus lies on researching and colonizing the Moon and Mars, as they are the closest celestial bodies to Earth. Understanding the resources available on these planets is paramount, as they may contain valuable minerals and substances that could benefit our planet and contribute to global prosperity. This exploration entails extensive scientific research to identify and utilize these resources effectively.

We require an array of natural resources such as uranium, iron, and gold from other planets to sustain prosperous life on Earth. Our agents, representing the International Intergalactical Space Secret Service, are committed to sourcing these resources with integrity and diligence. The agency was established through the collaboration of six nations:

the USA, Russia, India, Germany, China, England, and Georgiy Sergeyevich Garbuz. These nations serve as leaders of the agency, fostering global unity and cooperation. Each member nation hosts its own agency, with the head of the agency serving as the country's president, enhancing the president's authority.

PROJECT LYUBOV AND THE PATH TO PEACE

The pursuit of power among nations has historically led to conflicts resulting in the loss of innocent lives. Millions suffer due to conflicts driven by the desire for power, as seen in events like the Russian-Ukrainian war, fueled by aspirations for dominance. Such conflicts not only result in financial losses, as seen in Russia's sanctions-induced economic strain, but also disrupt global trade, leading to inflation and widespread challenges in resource procurement and transportation.

However, through the Project Lyubov, efforts are underway to achieve peace. A peace treaty, slated for completion by the year 2030, aims to resolve conflicts and foster harmony among nations, alleviating the suffering caused by power struggles and facilitating global prosperity.

This project is aimed at bringing peace and prosperity to Ukraine, Russia, and the entire world. However, its success depends on the willingness of each country to participate and enact change. Achieving peace between Russia and Ukraine is crucial for the establishment of the International Intergalactical Space Secret Service, an organization dedicated to providing humanitarian aid during planetary conflicts. The agency's mission includes evacuating children and civilians from dangerous areas to ensure their safety, making societal well-being its ultimate goal.

As we embark on space projects, the agency will focus on developing technologies to ensure the safety of human explorers and constructing habitats suitable for long-term habitation, equipped with essential resources such as air and water. Our fight is not against governments but for their cooperation in directing taxes toward free healthcare, education, and military expenses. We advocate for the establishment of space school academies and universities, leading to the formation of the International Intergalactical Space Federation.

Today, we stand as a testament to the future. If you share our vision, we invite you to join our cause. Together, we fight for the children, for love, and for a brighter tomorrow. In a world plagued by war and suffering, let us unite in love for our country, our people, and especially our children. Our motto, "Za Detey - For Kids. Za Lyubov - For Love. Live, Make, & Enjoy," embodies our commitment to a better future.

Sincerely and with warm regards,
Georgiy Sergeyevich Garbuz
Author

Shadow
Georgiy Sergeyevich Garbuz
2007

Debra
Georgiy Sergeyevich Garbuz
2007

Irina
Georgiy Sergeyevich Garbuz
2007

Two Dancers
Georgiy Sergeyevich Garbuz
2008

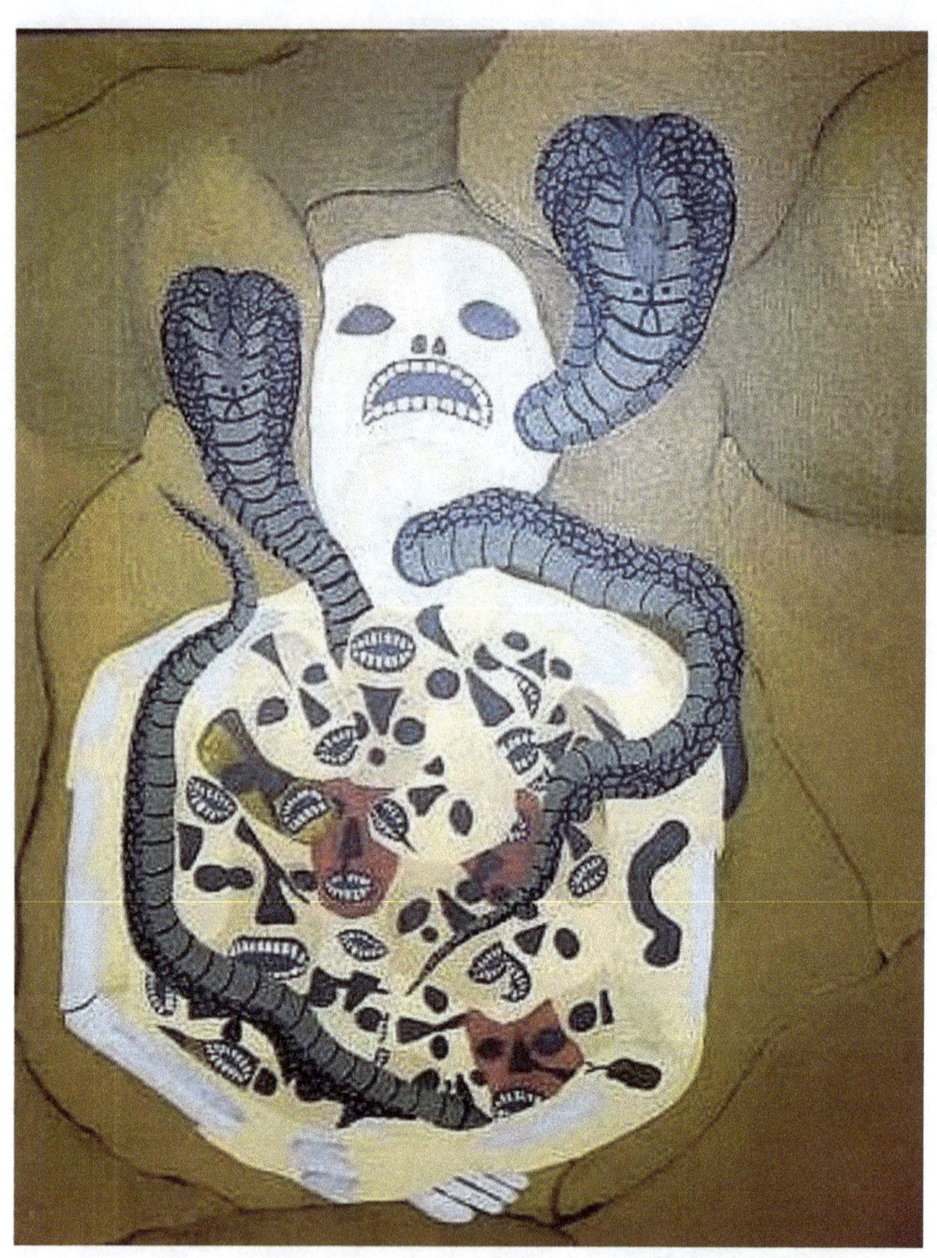

Death Feels
Georgiy Sergeyevich Garbuz
2007

Lovers
Georgiy Sergeyevich Garbuz
2008

Karnaval
Georgiy Sergeyevich Garbuz
2007

Geometry
Georgiy Sergeyevich Garbuz
2010

Angel with Two Slaves
Georgiy Sergeyevich Garbuz
2013

Gov
Georgiy Sergeyevich Garbuz
2010

Mirror
Georgiy Sergeyevich Garbuz
2008

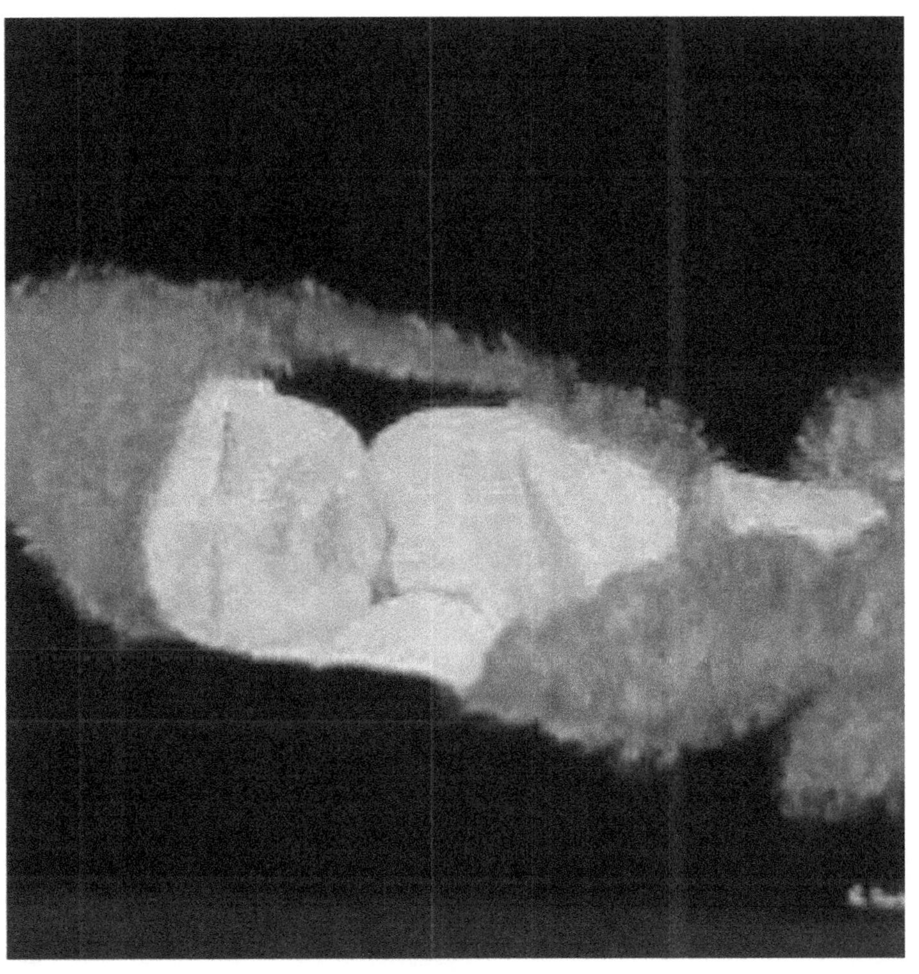

Erica
Georgiy Sergeyevich Garbuz
2010

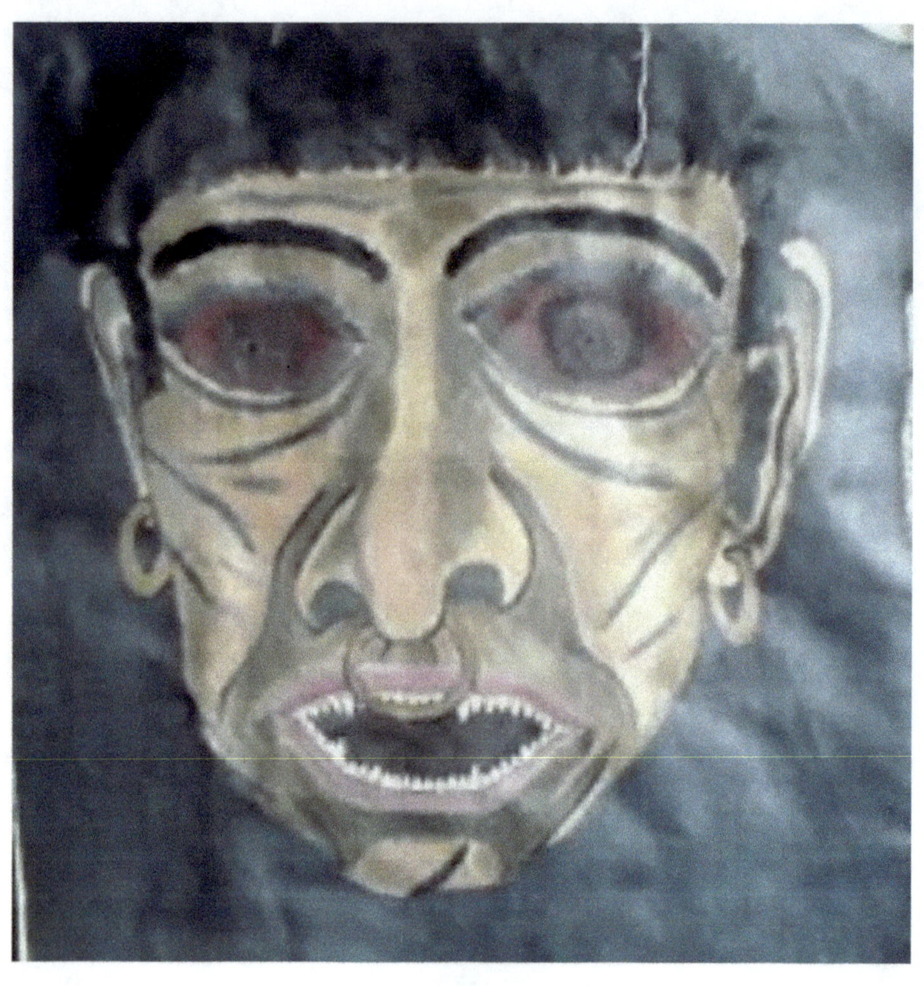

Blood
Georgiy Sergeyevich Garbuz
2011

Home
Georgiy Sergeyevich Garbuz
2011

Sister
Georgiy Sergeyevich Garbuz
2012

Sleep Baby
Georgiy Sergeyevich Garbuz
2014

Marry Me
Georgiy Sergeyevich Garbuz
2013

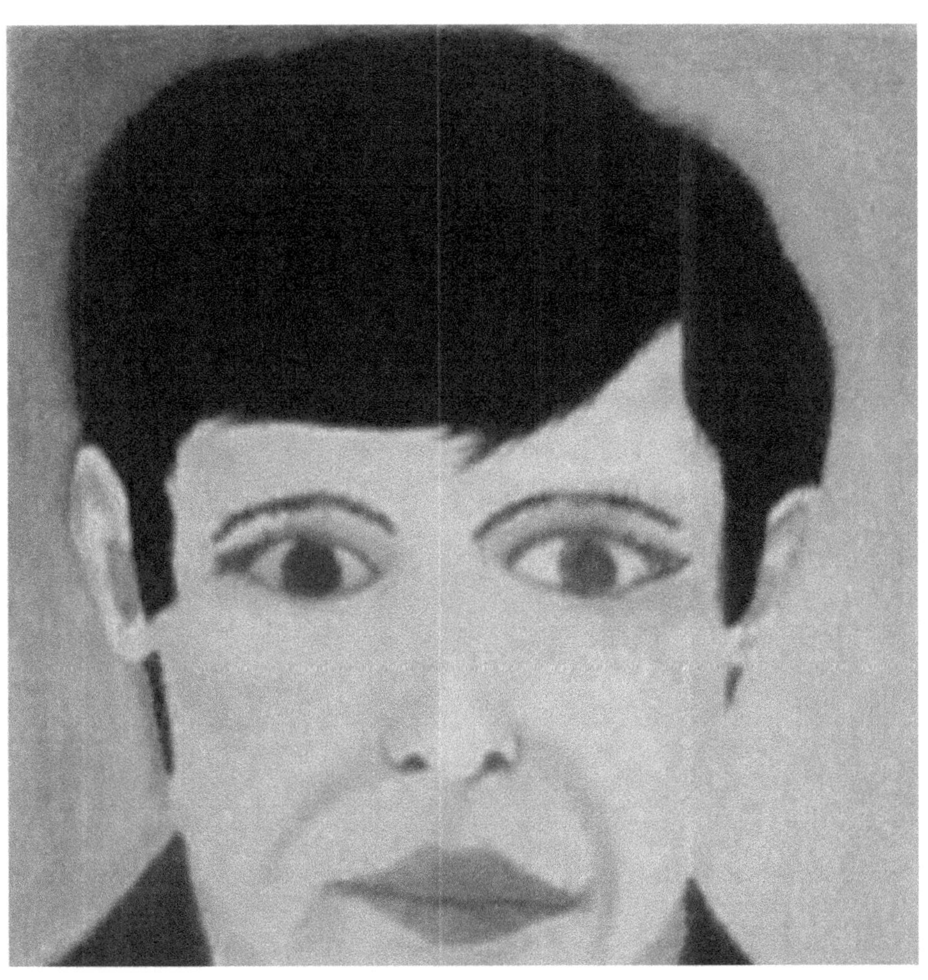

Serena
Georgiy Sergeyevich Garbuz
2013

Erika Fly
Georgiy Sergeyevich Garbuz
2020

Lyubov
Georgiy Sergeyevich Garbuz
2014

Lady
Georgiy Sergeyevich Garbuz
2014

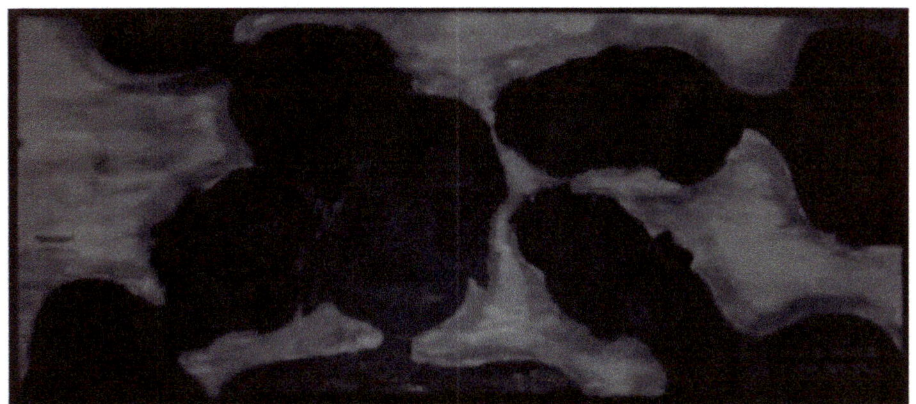

Crazy Aliens 1
Georgiy Sergeyevich Garbuz
2020

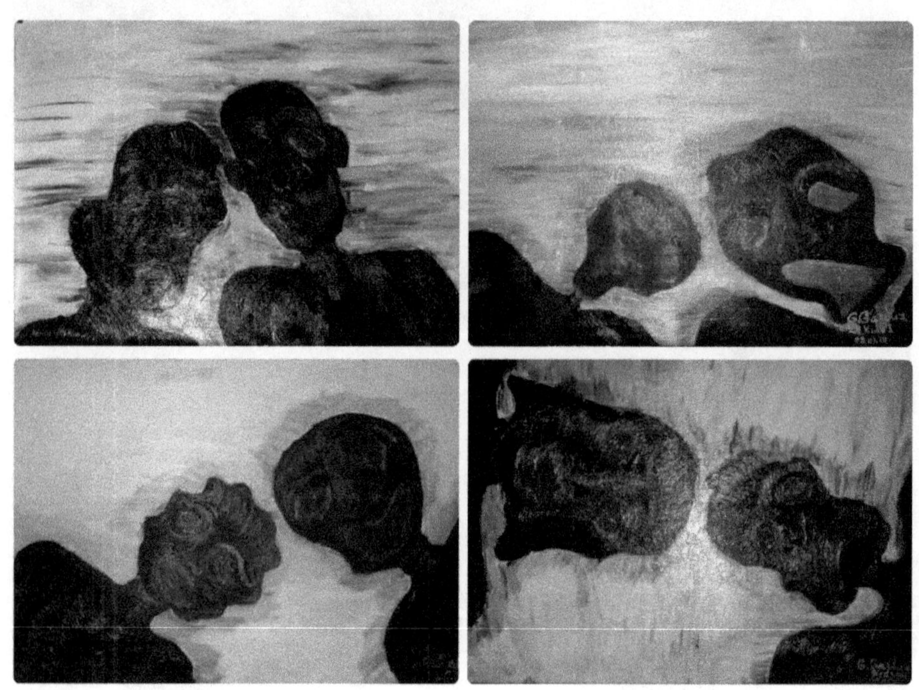

Crazy Aliens 2
Georgiy Sergeyevich Garbuz
2020

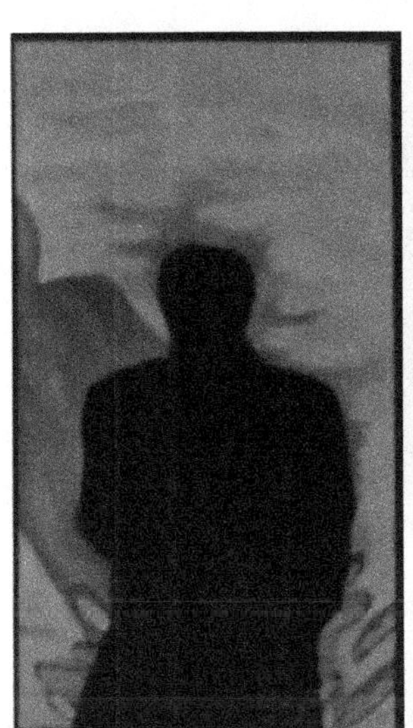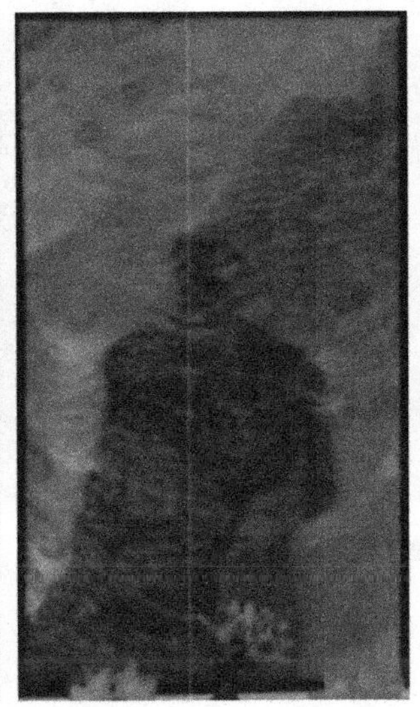

Winter Shadow
Georgiy Sergeyevich Garbuz
2020

Kid
Georgiy Sergeyevich Garbuz
2020

Down Town Minneapolis
Georgiy Sergeyevich Garbuz
2020

Sailor
Georgiy Sergeyevich Garbuz
2020

Storm
Georgiy Sergeyevich Garbuz
2020

Erika Ivonne
Georgiy Sergeyevich Garbuz
2020

Center of Eye
Georgiy Sergeyevich Garbuz
2021

Vera
Georgiy Sergeyevich Garbuz
2021

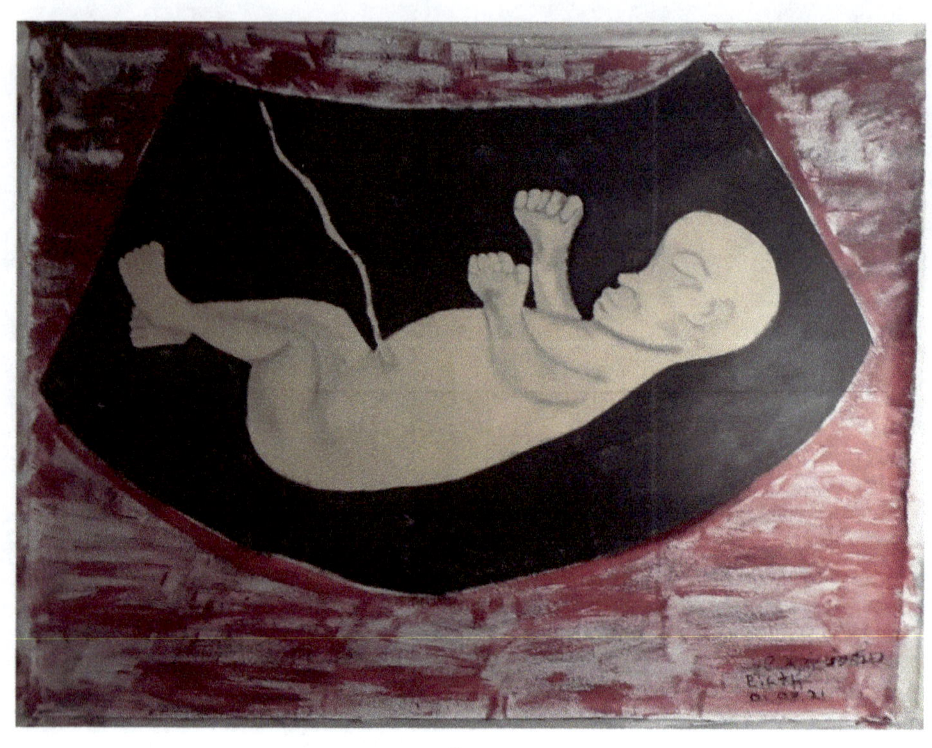

Born
Georgiy Sergeyevich Garbuz
2021

Lady
Georgiy Sergeyevich Garbuz
2021

Invitation to Heaven
Georgiy Sergeyevich Garbuz
2022

Smile
Georgiy Sergeyevich Garbuz
2022

Happiness
Georgiy Sergeyevich Garbuz
2022

Happy 1Shadow Georgiy
Sergeyevich Garbuz 2007

Georgiy Sergeyevich Garbuz
2022

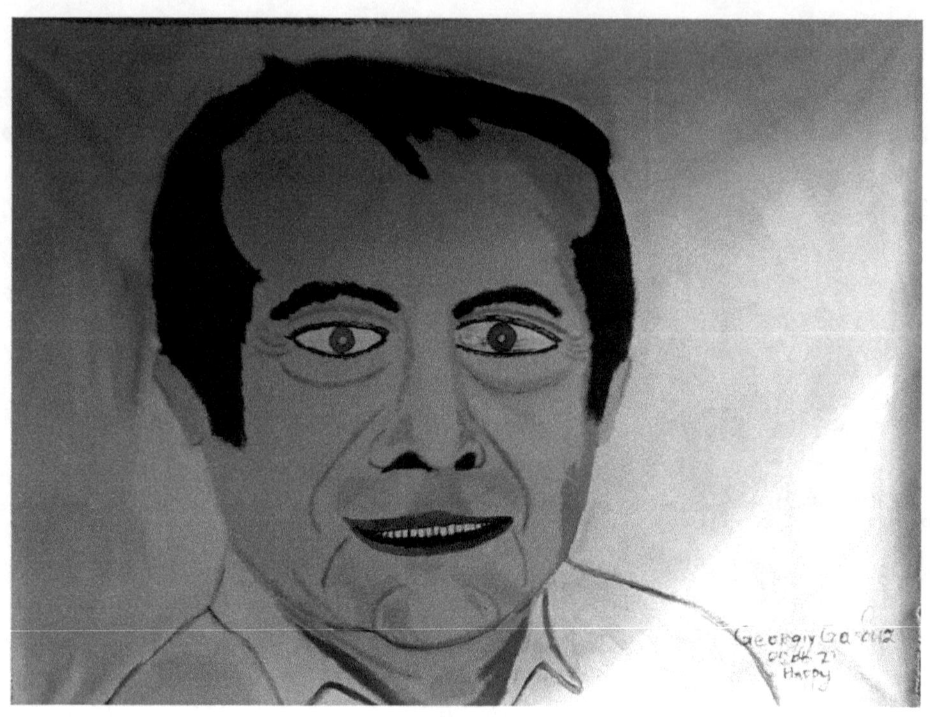

Happy 2
Georgiy Sergeyevich Garbuz
2021

Eagle Eye
Georgiy Sergeyevich Garbuz
2022

Lyubov Garbuz
Emily Taylor
2021